HENRY COLE

JACK'S GARDEN

GREENWILLOW BOOKS, NEW YORK

The full-color art was created with colored pencils on paper of different colors. The text type is Garamond.

Jack's Garden
Copyright © 1995 by Henry Cole. All rights reserved. Printed in Hong Kong by South China Printing Company (1988) Ltd.
www.harperchildrens.com
First Edition 10 9

Library of Congress Cataloging-in-Publication Data
Cole, Henry. Jack's garden/by Henry Cole.
    p.   cm.   "Greenwillow Books."
Summary: Cumulative text and illustrations depict what happens in Jack's garden after he plants his seeds.

ISBN 0-688-13501-3 (trade)
ISBN 0-688-15283-X (pbk.)
[1. Gardening—Fiction.] I. Title.
PZ7.C67345Jac 1995   [E]—dc20
94—6249 CIP AC

GARDEN CLAW

PRUNING SHEARS

This is the garden

that Jack planted.

TROWEL

RAKE

HOSE

SHOVEL

HOE

WATERING
CAN

EARTHWORMS

SLUG

This is the soil

that made up the garden

that Jack planted.

STAR-NOSED
MOLE

GROUND BEETLE

FLY PUPA

BEETLE LARVA

SLUG EGGS

MOTH LARVA

CICADA LARVA

CICADA

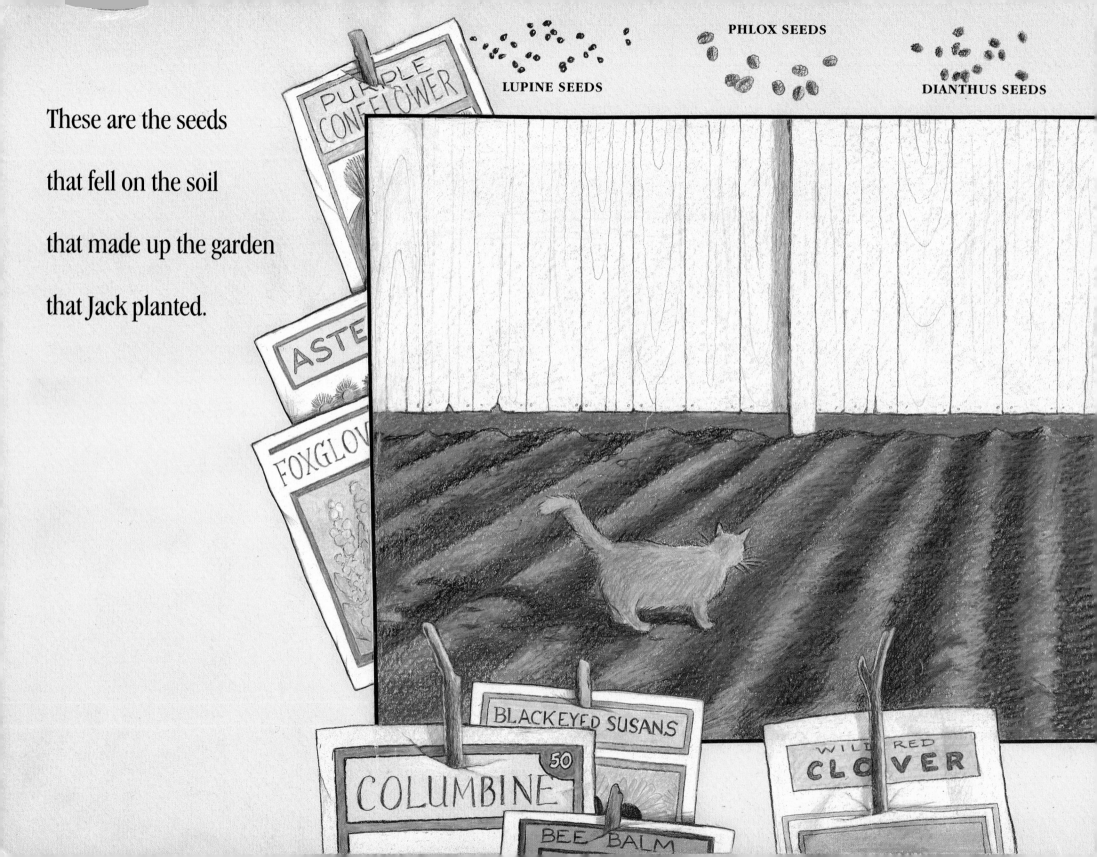

These are the seeds

that fell on the soil

that made up the garden

that Jack planted.

LUPINE SEEDS

PHLOX SEEDS

DIANTHUS SEEDS

PURPLE CONEFLOWER

ASTER

FOXGLOVE

BLACK EYED SUSANS

COLUMBINE

50

BEE BALM

WILD RED CLOVER

HOLLYHOCK SEEDS

POPPY SEEDS

SUNFLOWER SEEDS

MILKWEED SEEDS

BLUET
WILDFLOWER
95¢

ALLIUM

YARROW

WILDFLOWER MIX

75¢

LUPINE
FLOWER SEED

COREOPSIS

MORNING GLORY

DAISIES

This is the rain

that wet the seeds

that fell on the soil

that made up the garden

that Jack planted.

STRATUS
CLOUD

CIRRUS
CLOUD

CIRROCUMULUS
CLOUD

RAIN
GAUGE

These are the seedlings

that sprouted with the rain

that wet the seeds

that fell on the soil

that made up the garden

that Jack planted.

SEED
LEAVES

ROOTS

STEM

CENTIPEDE

MILLIPEDE

ADULT
LEAVES

SEED
LEAVES

ROOTS

ROBIN

SOW BUG

GERMINATING
SEED

These are the plants

that grew from the seedlings

that sprouted with the rain

that wet the seeds

that fell on the soil

that made up the garden

that Jack planted.

BEE
BALM

ALLIUM

HOLLYHOCK

ARGIOPE
SPIDER

GOLDENROD
SPIDER

SWALLOWTAIL
LARVA

LACEWING

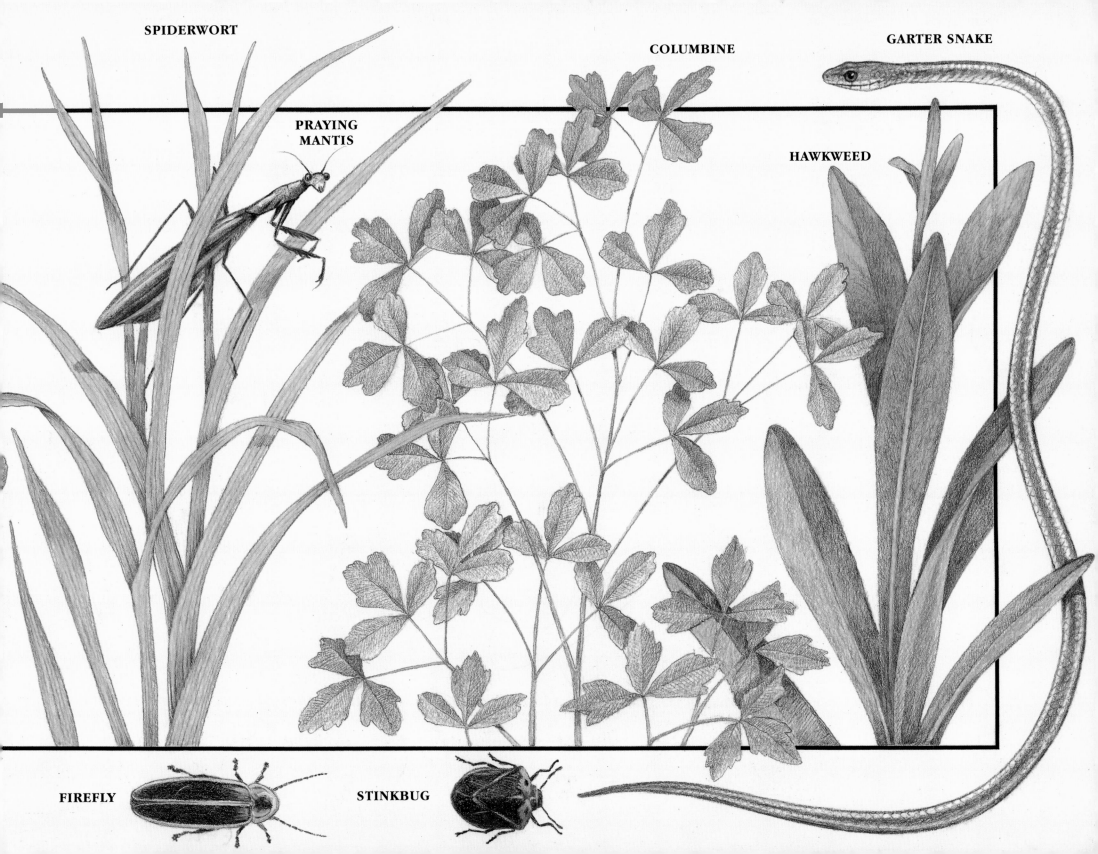

SPIDERWORT

PRAYING
MANTIS

COLUMBINE

GARTER SNAKE

HAWKWEED

FIREFLY

STINKBUG

These are the buds

that formed on the plants

that grew from the seedlings

that sprouted with the rain

that wet the seeds

that fell on the soil

that made up the garden

that Jack planted.

LADYBIRD BEETLE LARVA

BUTTERCUP

DIANTHUS

FOXGLOVE

2-SPOTTED LADYBIRD BEETLE

VARIABLE LADYBIRD BEETLE

CONVERGENT LADYBIRD BEETLE

9-SPOTTED LADYBIRD BEETLE

POPPY

PHLOX

LADYBIRD BEETLE EGGS

7-SPOTTED LADYBIRD BEETLE

MILKWEED

TWICE-STABBED LADYBIRD BEETLE

SPOTTED LADYBIRD BEETLE

ASHY GRAY LADYBIRD BEETLE

WILLOW LEAF BEETLE

These are the flowers

that blossomed from the buds

that formed on the plants

that grew from the seedlings

that sprouted with the rain

that wet the seeds

that fell on the soil

that made up the garden

that Jack planted.

ASTER

BLACK-EYED SUSAN

LUPINE

RED
CLOVER

WHITE CLOVER

FLEABANE

WILD GERANIUM

YARROW

MULLEIN

COREOPSIS

BEE
BALM

PINKS

BLUET

SPIDERWORT

DAISY

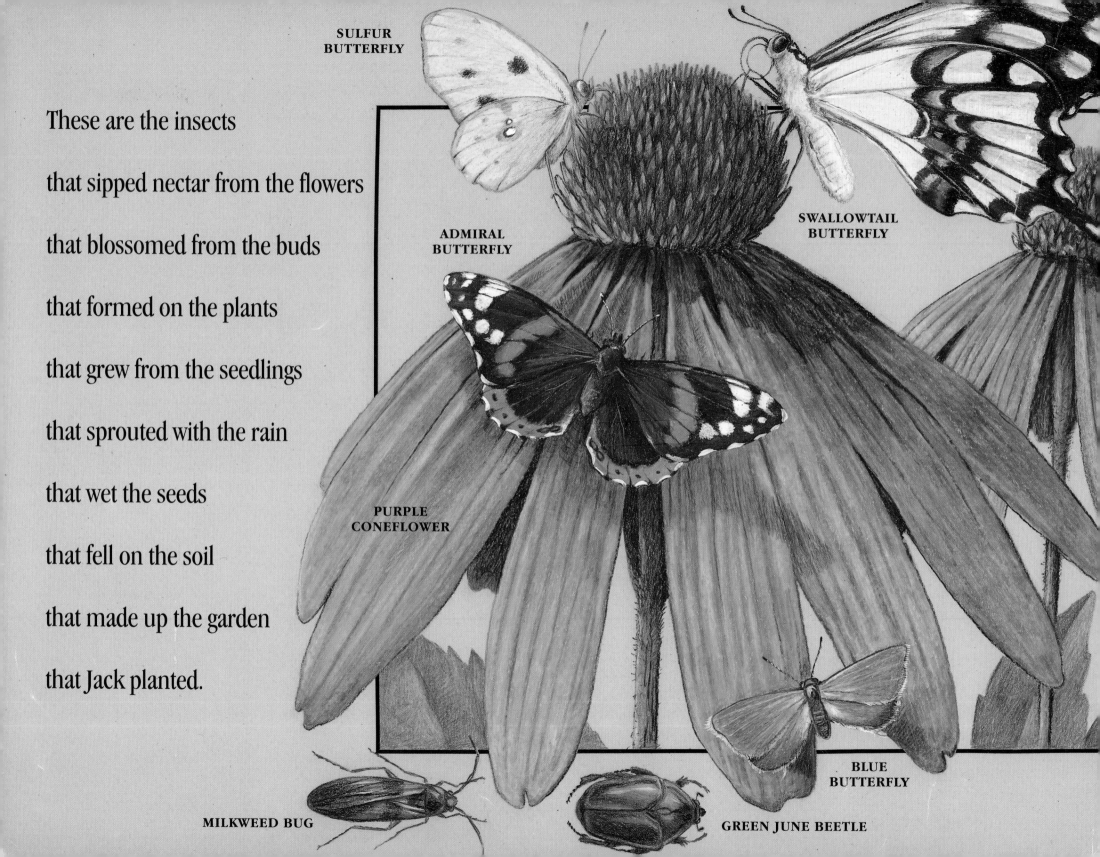

These are the insects

that sipped nectar from the flowers

that blossomed from the buds

that formed on the plants

that grew from the seedlings

that sprouted with the rain

that wet the seeds

that fell on the soil

that made up the garden

that Jack planted.

SULFUR
BUTTERFLY

ADMIRAL
BUTTERFLY

SWALLOWTAIL
BUTTERFLY

PURPLE
CONEFLOWER

BLUE
BUTTERFLY

MILKWEED BUG

GREEN JUNE BEETLE

SOLDIER BEETLE

SKIPPER BUTTERFLY

SARA ORANGE TIP
BUTTERFLY

BUMBLEBEE

BUCKEYE
BUTTERFLY

LONG-HORNED BEETLE

COPPER BUTTERFLY

METALLIC
BEE

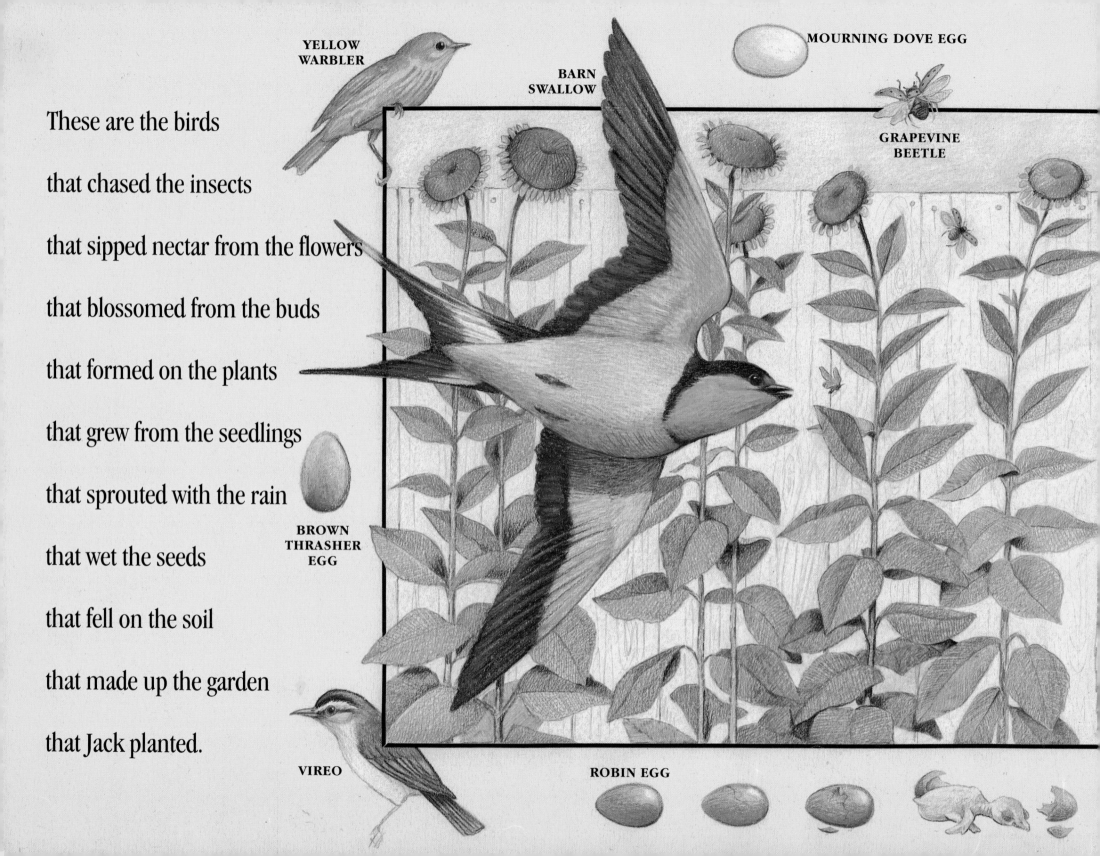

These are the birds

that chased the insects

that sipped nectar from the flowers

that blossomed from the buds

that formed on the plants

that grew from the seedlings

that sprouted with the rain

that wet the seeds

that fell on the soil

that made up the garden

that Jack planted.

YELLOW
WARBLER

BARN
SWALLOW

MOURNING DOVE EGG

GRAPEVINE
BEETLE

BROWN
THRASHER
EGG

VIREO

ROBIN EGG

YELLOW
WARBLER EGG

GOLDFINCH EGG

CATBIRD

VIREO
EGG

SUNFLOWERS

BLUEBIRD
EGG

BLUEBIRD

BARN
SWALLOW
EGG

CATBIRD EGG

GOLDFINCH

MORNING
GLORY

MOURNING
DOVE

And this is the garden

that Jack planted.

BROWN
THRASHER

HUMMINGBIRD

TO START YOUR OWN GARDEN,

find a spot where you may dig. Your mom or dad may need to help you get started. Choose a place that gets some sunshine and isn't too wet.

Hardware stores and supermarkets sell all kinds of seeds. Or you can order seeds through the mail: Try W. Atlee Burpee Seed Company (300 Park Avenue, Warminster, PA 18974) or Park Seed Company (Cokesbury Road, Greenwood, SC 29647).

The seeds you get may be very delicate, so handle them carefully. They shouldn't be planted deeply in the soil. Here's a good way to plant very tiny seeds, like poppy seeds: Put some soil in a bowl or pan and gently mix the seeds in with it. Then scatter the seeded soil over the ground. After planting or scattering the seeds, water them gently.

(Or maybe you'll be lucky like Jack and have a spring shower do the watering!)

Some plants like sunnier spots, some like shadier places. Look at the backs of the seed packets to find out which are best for different parts of your garden. Black-eyed Susans, for example, like it nice and sunny. Spiderwort likes it shady and moist.

Some plants are tall, some are short. Most of the time the seed packet will tell you how tall that plant will become. Put tall plants at the back of your garden and short ones up front.

Some plants bloom in the spring, like foxglove, and some later in the summer, like hollyhocks. You can grow different kinds of plants so that something will be blooming all season.

A good place to get more information on starting a garden is your local County Extension Office or your library.

Happy Gardening!